Everyone Knows What a Dragon Looks Like

written by Jay Williams

illustrated by Mercer Mayer

FOUR WINDS PRESS   NEW YORK

Four Winds Press
Macmillan Publishing Company
866 Third Avenue, New York, NY 10022
Collier Macmillan Canada, Inc.

Printed in the United States of America

10   9   8   7   6   5   4

Library of Congress Cataloging in Publication Data

Williams, Jay.
    Everyone knows what a dragon looks like.

    SUMMARY: Because of the road sweeper's belief in him,
a dragon saves the city of Wu from the Wild Horsemen of
the north.

    [1. Dragons – Fiction.   2. China – Fiction]   I. Mayer,
Mercer, illus.   II. Title.
PZ7. W666EV [E]   74-13121
ISBN 0-02-793090-4

Everyone Knows
What a Dragon Looks Like

he city of Wu was perched on a hill between two moun-
tains. On one side of it were the great plains of the north
where the Wild Horsemen lived. On the other side was
the land of China.

A lad named Han was the gate-sweeper of the city. He had no mother or father and he was very poor. He lived in a tiny hut next to the gate, and his job was to sweep the road that ran through the gate. For this, he was given one bowl of rice and one cup of wine every day, and that was all he had. But he was cheerful, kind-hearted and friendly, and when he swept the road he whistled. Everyone who went in or out of the city had a merry word from him, for that was all he had to give.

One day, a messenger came racing along the road from the north. He said to Han, "Take me to the ruler of the city."

Han led him to the palace of the Mandarin, the great lord whose name was Jade Tiger.

The messenger cried, "Beware! The Wild Horsemen of the north are coming, a great army of them. They mean to destroy the city of Wu and bring war into the land of China."

The Mandarin stroked his beard. Then he called together his councilors. They were the Leader of the Merchants, the Captain of the Army, the Wisest of the Wise Men, and the Chief of the Workmen.

"What shall we do?" asked the Mandarin.

"There are four things we can do," answered the Wise Man. "First, we can fight."

"Our army is small," said the Captain. "They know how to shout loudly, how to make threatening leaps, and how to wave their swords in the bravest possible way. But they don't know much about fighting."

"Well, then, secondly we can run away from the city," said the Wise Man.

"If we run into the land of China, the Emperor will cut off our heads," said the Leader of the Merchants.

"Thirdly," said the Wise Man, "we can surrender."

"If we surrender, the Wild Horsemen will cut off our heads," remarked the Chief Workman.

"What is the fourth thing?" asked the Mandarin.

The Wise Man shrugged. "We can pray to the Great Cloud Dragon to help us."

"That seems most practical," said the Mandarin.

So the gongs were beaten, and the smoke of sweet incense rose up while everyone in the city prayed.

The next morning, as Han was sweeping the road under the gate, a small, fat man came walking up the hill. He had a long white beard and a shiny bald head, and he leaned on a long staff.

"Good morning," he said.

Han bowed. "I hope your honorable stomach is happy, sir," he replied, politely.

"Will you take me to the ruler of the city?" said the little fat man.

"I'll take you to him," said Han, "but he is very busy this morning. We are expecting the enemy, and the Mandarin is praying to the Great Cloud Dragon for help."

"I know," said the little man. "I am a dragon."

Han opened his eyes very wide. "You don't look like one," he said.

"How do you know?" asked the little man. "Have you ever seen one?"

"No," said Han. "Now that you mention it, I haven't."

"Well, then—?"

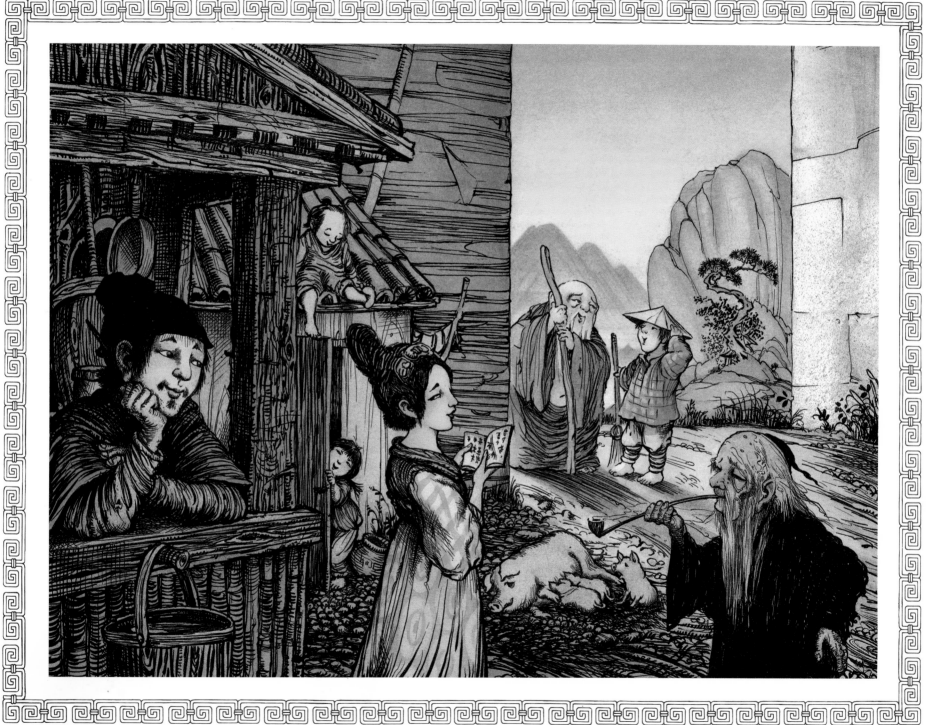

"Well, then," said Han, "please come this way, Honorable Dragon."

He led the little fat man to the palace. There sat the Mandarin with his councilors. They had just finished a huge bowl of rice and six dozen duck eggs for breakfast and they were drinking their tea.

The Mandarin looked at the little fat man with a frown.

"Who is this person and why have you brought him here?" he asked Han.

"Sir," said Han, "he is a dragon."

"Don't be ridiculous," said the Mandarin. "He's a fat man who is tracking dirt on my fine carpets. What do you want here, old man?"

"I have come to help you," said the little fat man. "But if you want a dragon to help you, you must treat him with courtesy. I have come a long, weary way. Give me something to eat and something to drink and speak to me politely, and I will save the city."

"Now, look here," said the Mandarin. "Everybody knows what dragons look like. They are proud lords of the sky. They wear gold and purple silk. They look like Mandarins."

"How do you know?" asked the little man. "Have you ever seen one?"

"Certainly not," said the Mandarin. "But everyone knows what they look like. Isn't that true, Captain?"

The Captain of the Army sat up straight, brushing grains of rice from his uniform.

"Not at all," said he. "Everyone knows that dragons are fierce and brave, like warriors. The sight of them is like the sound of trumpets. They look like Captains of the Army."

"Nonsense!" interrupted the Leader of the Merchants. "Dragons are rich and splendid. They are as comfortable as a pocketful of money. They look like merchants. Everyone knows that."

The Chief of the Workmen put in, "You are wrong. Everyone knows that dragons are strong and tough. Nothing is too hard for them to do. They look like workmen."

The Wisest of the Wise Men pushed his glasses up on his forehead. "The one thing that is known—and indeed I can show it to you in forty-seven books—is that dragons are the wisest of all creatures," he said. "Therefore, they must look like wise men."

At that moment, they heard screams and yells from outside. A messenger came running into the palace.

"My lords," he shouted, "the enemy is coming! The Wild Horsemen are riding across the plain toward the city gates. What shall we do?"

Everyone rushed out to the gate to look. Far away, but coming closer every second, was the dark mass of horsemen. Dust rose high from their horses' hoofs and their swords and spears twinkled in the sunlight.

The little fat man stood quietly leaning on his staff. "If you will treat me with courtesy," he said, "I will save the city. Give me something to eat and something to drink and speak to me politely. That is the only way to get a dragon to help you."

"Piffle and poffle!" cried the Mandarin. "You are not a dragon! Everyone can see that you are only a dusty old wanderer. We have no time to give you free meals or to talk politely. Get out of the way."

And he ran home to the palace and crawled under the bed where he lay shivering.

"My gallant army," commanded the Captain, "follow me!"

He turned and ran to the barracks and all his soldiers followed him. They all hid under their beds and lay there shaking.

The Merchant, the Wise Man, and the Chief of the Workmen fled to their own houses and all the people hurried after them. In a few minutes, the streets were empty except for Han and the little fat old man.

"Well," said Han, "I don't think we have much time. The enemy will be here soon. I don't know whether you are a dragon or not, but if you are hungry and thirsty, please do me the honor of coming into my humble house."

With a low bow he showed the old man the way into his tiny hut. There, he gave him the bowl of rice and the cup of wine which were all he had.

The old man ate and drank. Then he stood up.

"I don't think much of the people of Wu," he said, "but for your sake I will save the city."

He went out to the gate. The Wild Horsemen were very close.
They wore fur caps and the skins of tigers. They shot arrows at
the city as they rode hard on their shaggy horses.

The little fat man puffed out his cheeks. He blew a long breath.
The sky grew dark and lightning sizzled from the clouds to the
earth. A great wind arose. It caught the Wild Horsemen and blew
them far and wide. Those who escaped turned and galloped
madly away through the storm.

The sky cleared. The sun shone again. The plain was empty.

The little fat man said, "Now I will show you what a dragon
looks like."

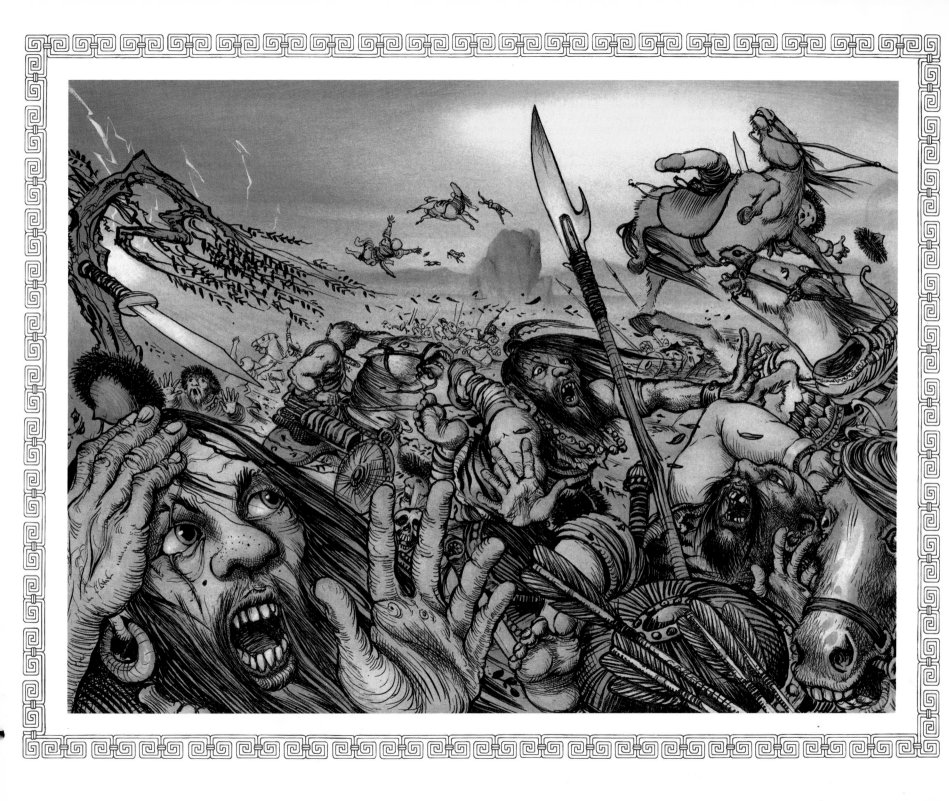

He sprang up into the air and his form changed. He grew taller than the tallest tree, taller than the tallest tower. He was the color of sunset shining through rain. Scales covered him, scattering light. His claws and teeth glittered like diamonds. His eyes were noble like those of a proud horse. He was more beautiful and more frightening than anything Han had ever seen.

He flew high, roaring, and vanished into the deep sky. Han gave a long sigh and went to tell the Mandarin what had happened.

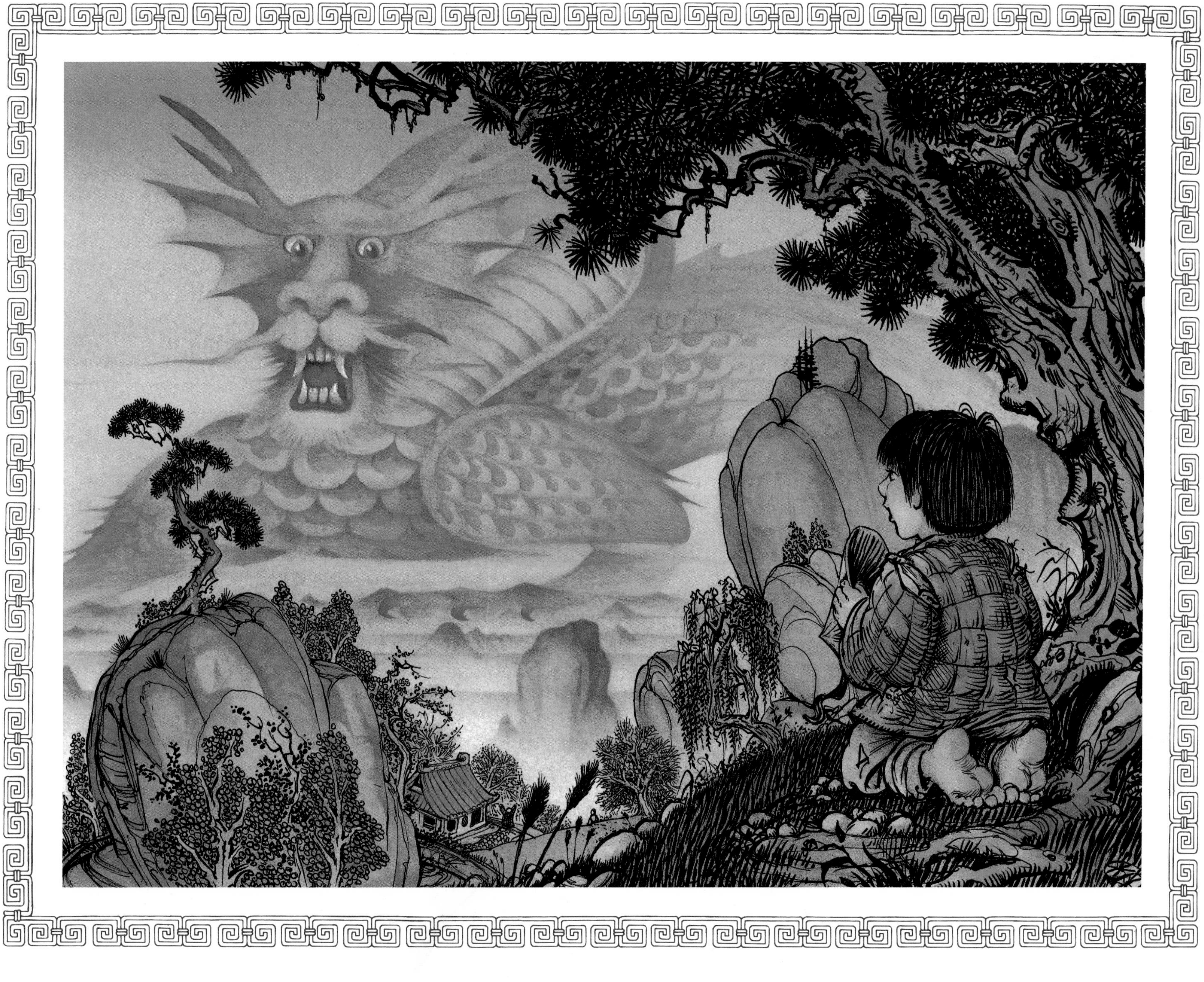

The people of the city crowded around to hear the tale. They could see for themselves that the enemy had vanished. They cheered Han, pinned medals on him, gave him many gold pieces, and from that day on called him "The Honorable Defender of the City."

"But best of all," said the Mandarin, "we know what a dragon looks like. He looks like a small, fat, bald old man."

The late JAY WILLIAMS wrote many award-winning children's books, including *The Practical Princess, Petronella,* and *The Reward Worth Having.* He is also well known for his books for middle-graders, including *The Magic Grandfather* and the popular "Danny Dunn" science fiction books.

MERCER MAYER is the author-illustrator of many books for young readers, including *What Do You Do With a Kangaroo?,* winner of the Brooklyn Art Books for Children Citation; *The Great Cat Chase;* and *East of the Sun & West of the Moon.* He is the author of the popular *Appelard and Liverwurst* (illustrated by Steven Kellogg), and the illustrator of *The Reward Worth Having* by Jay Williams, and *Beauty and the Beast,* retold by Marianna Mayer. He lives with his wife, Jo, and their two children in Connecticut.

What the Critics Say about
EVERYONE KNOWS WHAT A DRAGON LOOKS LIKE

Selected as one of the Nine Best Illustrated Children's Books of the Year, 1976, *New York Times Book Review*

Selected as one of the Ten Best Children's Books of the Year, 1977, *Learning* magazine

---

A 1976 AIGA Children's Book Show Selection

Irma Simonton Black Award, 1976

"Perhaps the most exquisite children's book of the current season."
— *Publishers Weekly*

"A wonderful tale with a sly humor that older readers as well as young listeners will enjoy. . . . Mayer's elegant line drawings and fun color artwork suggest both Oriental delicacy and the vitality of robust folk humor."   — ★*School Library Journal*

"Illustrations in this Oriental tale are exquisite; beautiful enough to frame."
— *Instructor*

"A fascinating tour de force of color and style."   — *The New York Times*

"A dramatic yet subtly mocking story heightened by ambitiously executed full-page illustrations, rich in the detail and coloring of Oriental tapestries."
— *ALA Booklist*